Kydee's Karma

D'Boy=FCKBoy

By

LaShawn Tait

General Information

Kydee's Karma

D'Boy=FCKBoy

LaShawn Tait

Cover Design: TP Graphics- Shantorya Jones

Publisher: B.O.S.S. Publishing, LLC

Editor: Terry L. Ware Sr.

ISBN: 978-0-9988341-3-9

1. Novel 2. Fiction 3. Nonfiction

First Edition

Thank You

I could thank a lot of people for being influencing factors in my life, but I will start at the very beginning by thanking my Heavenly Father for blessing me with the gift of life and for this heart of all hearts.

I also want to thank my family for being my support, Ma Dukes(Chinnie), thank you for not giving up on me. Jas, Dmack, Mykel, my Princess TiChina, Jameson and DJ all my love.

I would also like to thank the men in my life who played instrumental parts whether it was advice or whatever I needed at the moment. My Bestie, Tory Thompson(Action), you are the best, you are life. Terry Ware Sr., the first time I heard you flow on the mic, you inspired me to do exactly what I did in this book, live through this paper and pen and to let my gift flow freely.

Emanuel(E), you have always kept it 1000 even if it hurt and that's what a true friend does.

Franklin(Slymm) and Jason(JB), my Dappa Donz the two of you have been my rocks, holding me down for years. Your advice helped to mold me into the Queen that I am today. Thanks Nick, you've become my best friend and I appreciate all that you do. Thanks friends and family, you all played your positions.

To the FCKBoy who inspired me to write this book, thank you for the lesson, because now I have learned to walk, no to run when boys like you come my way. Thank you for the gift of flight, because now I'm a Phoenix who has learned to fly high above the fuckeries of life and all its lies.

~Kydee Karma~

Table of Contents

Kydee's Karma

D'Boy=FCKBoy

By

LaShawn Tait

Prologue

Today I make this pen cry, not just for me but for all females like me. All the ones who love with every being in their bodies and who also give their hearts to the very men who ultimately reveal themselves to be a D'Boy/FCKBoy.

Men, if you are not ready to commit yourself to the woman whom you confess your undying love to on the daily, then please don't abuse or mistreat her heart with the lies and the fuckery. You see, when you dishrag, (play with a person's emotions knowing you have no intentions of building with them but you lead them on with words of deception just because you can), please believe Karma always comes back and wreaks chaos and trust me, it's well deserved.

Ladies please allow me the chance to enlighten you on my experience with what I have finally realized was nothing more than a FCKBoy.

1

Karma has a way of presenting itself at the very moment when you think that everything is all rainbows, peaches and cream, and happy ever after. So, trust me I wasn't prepared when she wrapped her hands around my throat and placed that invisible padlock with a matching ball and chain to hold me down, especially after 16 years of dealing with the same man off and on but yeah, that trick caught me. Always remember that no matter what you do in life, the good and the bad, what I can guarantee is that you get that energy back, there's no escape.

As I prepare to take you down memory lane, here's your opportunity to walk away, especially if you can't handle blood raw and uncut facts, but if you are willing to embrace this truth and accept this gift of knowledge that I am giving you, then perhaps you can save yourself a lot of heart ache and pain in the future. Then and only then will you be able to avoid a FCKBoy at all costs. I just wish someone would have given me this 411 (information) early in the game, things would have ended up so much differently. Lesson well learned though, despite everything else. This is not a situation where I will bash D'Boy because truth be told I had much love for him, it was the person who I later found out he was that made me come to this sad, sad reality. He was a FCKBoy from the gate (beginning).

Chapter 1

You see me and Kydee met over a decade ago, he was a friend of the family and though I was in a lesbian relationship with Patron, I always thought Kydee was sexy as hell. Kydee was younger than me but he had hella swag. Yeah, I won't lie, I wanted him, but maybe one day.

I never really put much effort into fulfilling those desires until years and years later. Kydee eventually got married and was doing his own thing and so was I, but I always wondered what if. Kydee left our little small town after her got married and moved to the "G" and I had no idea that our paths would cross again or that I would ultimately give him the innermost part of my soul and my heart, but it was destined for these things to transpire. They made me into this Queen who is about to open your eyes to the real.

Kydee and his wife were having problems and I was fresh out of a long-term relationship with Patron and I also recently had moved to the "G'" with a cousin who I won't lie, also use to have feelings for Kydee. Yeah, I know, but Karma eventually made a fool out of me for that shit.

Getting off work one day and walking to the apartment I heard someone calling my name, I'm new to this place and no one knows me. So, I turn around slowly and guess who it is, it's Kydee. I'm happy to see him and we exchange numbers, of course I'm not expecting to hear from him, but he texts me later that night. After multiple texts and phone calls we finally decided to hook up and spend a little time together. I mean we had talked so much shit on the phone it was time to see if this lil youngsta could back it up.

So, the day slowly progresses into night and I've psyched myself up because he's coming over in a few hours. Damn the mood was right and then mother nature decided to make a visit.

Yes, that should have been a red flag, one of many that I would get throughout this situation, all of which I ignored of course. It's way too late to call and cancel but maybe he will just come over, we chill, maybe watch a movie, or just talk. Hmmmmm, this will be my way of getting out of having sex because I'm nervous as hell anyway and I'm not sure if I'm ready to give in and have sex with him yet.

Doorbell rings, I'm fresh out the shower with a black tank and some black Adidas (ALL DAY I DREAM ABOUT SEX) shorts, now ain't that shit ironic. When I open the door Kydee's cologne was so erotic and sensual I could feel his presence in places that he didn't need to be. All I could say was damnnnnnnnn. You see Kydee is from New York with bowlegs and beautiful skin and well let me continue.

We sit on the couch as Kydee rolls up a blunt, we both smoking and I'm hoping that this will calm my nerves and maybe take the edge off.

Of course, it mellows me out but I'm still kind of nervous. I can't get still and Kydee is laughing because he knows that this sexual tension between us is getting the best of me. I'm shaking, and he keeps holding me down asking me if I'm goodie. I'm smiling and smoking trying to maintain my composure. Kydee leans over and kisses me. I try to back away but shit, he got some major skills.

His tongue is stroking the inside of my cheeks and he's making it roll against mine, fuccccccck! He's kissing and licking all down my neck and biting all down my shoulders and my back. Damn, as much as I want him I can't do this, wrong time of the month. He keeps trying to slide his hand between my legs and I'm telling him noooooo, knowing damn well if he keeps this up he's about to find this tampon string in a minute.

He gets down on the floor and starts to kiss and lick on my thighs and I'm hella aroused but I know I need to stop this, but I can't. He's rolling his tongue like a snake and I'm literally about to lose my mind. I lay back on the sofa and for a split second, I kinda give in and he manages to slide his hands through the pants leg of my shorts and he finds the string. I'm embarrassed but he just looks at me and says, "OH, so is this what you were worried about?"

He gets up, walks into the kitchen, and returns with a paper towel. He pulls out the tampon and takes it and places it in the trash and comes back and says. "Ma, I'm gonna float on the top, I got my red wings." The mere shock of his actions and words did not prepare me for anything that took place afterwards and well, please brace yourself for those details. Kydee took me to a place I had never gone before.

So, as he proceeded to feast on my cookie like it was his last meal, he kept flicking his tongue on my clit so fast that I climbed the wall like Spider-Woman. He was aggressive as hell too and I absolutely loved that shit, the more I ran the more he grabbed me and told me to bring that ass

8

back and that's just what I did, I brought it back to him. Damn, I can't take this, but ohhhhhhhh it feels so good, I don't want him to stop. The more he licked and sucked on my clit the more I grinded my cookie into his face, legs wrapped around his neck and he's moaning into my cookie telling me how good it was and I'm begging him not to stop and then, 1 orgasm, then 2, then 3, then skeet skeet skeet.

After Kydee was finished with me I pushed him back on the couch and I gently French kissed the tip of that beautiful curved penis. I swear it's so smooth and it smells as good as it tasted. Kydee had some skills with that tongue but now it's time for me to show him exactly what I'm about. He had his red wings but trust me I snatch souls and I'm definitely a cannibal.

I took Kydee and swallowed him inch by inch rolling my tongue down that dick until he decided he just wanted to fuck my throat, so he grabbed me by my head and did just that. He straight fucked my mouth, guess he thought I was going to gag, but of course I didn't, and when he busted in my mouth I refused to stop sucking so I swallowed millions probably billions of the little souls coming from him.

Kydee wasn't finished and snatched me up off the floor and pushed me on my back and when I told him no, he told me, "you might as well give me this pussy, hell we've done everything else." When he entered me for the first time, I swear I fell in love. As I was biting into his shoulder and as he was making love to me, all I could do to keep from telling him that I loved him was to bite and suck a little bit harder on his neck and I swear it's like we were in a marathon. We sexed until the next morning.

You see, I know what you're thinking, damn they are nasty as hell, but reality is, I've always had control of my period especially when I wanted to fuck, I could make it come to a complete stop, so glad I did, I think I just fell in love. That was the night that he actually swallowed my soul, LITERALLY!

Our night went on until the next day and when he left, my confusion was at an all-time high. Did that shit just happen or was it all just a figment of my imagination? My body and mind were both exhausted, so I fell asleep not having any idea of how I could remotely process what just transpired. I just need to sleep this shit off, it's the weekend, I'm off work and I have the place to myself, so I'm just going to clean up.

Notification goes off on my phone, it's a message from Kydee asking me if I was goodie and how he enjoyed kicking it with me last night. Hmmmmm, so did I but I can't believe we… So, I continue to clean, and another message comes through. "When can I see you again?" Well damn, after last night whenever you want to.

We decided to keep in touch not knowing that our night together would ultimately be the beginning of a 16-year situationship (a situation between two people that has the characteristics of being a relationship, but reality is it doesn't have a label on it). The more Kydee and I saw each other I kind of forgot that he was married. We were so bold with what we were doing. He would drop me off at work and drive my car home. My lack of respect for his wife was obvious because I would call the house phone and ask her to speak to him. All the time Karma was taking notes and just waiting. Me, I didn't care I just wanted him.

<u>*Lesson 1*</u>

If he doesn't care about how his actions will affect the woman he stood in front of God, and man, and said vows to honor, love, protect, and forsake all others and then say I DO! Then trust me, he's a FCKBoy! If he's not loyal to his wife, he sure as hell isn't the one for you, and he knows nothing of loyalty at all.

Chapter 2

Sad thing about it is that I didn't realize what I had gotten myself into. You see I've had multiple encounters with multiple men, but I swear there was always something different about Kydee. The way he texted was even a turn on, his verbiage and the darkness of his soul drew me closer and closer to him each and every single day, like a moth to a never-ending flame. You see Kydee is a gifted man but without the guidance of a true Queen he will never reach his full potential, therefore, his FCKBoy tendencies will always supersede his gifts and talents.

Like myself he writes poetry that will take you on a visual journey into the mind of a soulless angel. Yeah, he had me, I was gone and the more time we spent together I fell head over heels in love with him. After picking Kydee up from home and dropping him off at work one day, Kydee got hurt at work and just hearing my baby crying and telling me that he needed me to come to the hospital, you know I had to go. I had to make sure that he was goodie.

Me and my girl Titto pull up, when we get there a couple family members were already there. I was telling him that I loved him and that I would check on him later and in walks his wife and her mother. It really wasn't a big deal to me, he never respected the situation so why should I? We prepare to leave, not because I'm scared, but because he was already in pain and I didn't want him to have to deal with any drama or make the situation any worse. No need to be scared when his wife knew what it was just like she knew who I was to him.

Titto and I walked to the elevator and just as the door is about to close the mother-in-law stops the doors from closing, asking us "which one of us is Kydee's mistress?" We both look at each other and start laughing, and I say, how can one have a mistress when there's no marriage? Damn, karma was still taking notes and yes, I'm going to see that trick one day soon but not today though, oh well.

Anyway, Kydee's injury and the fact that he loved his weeji (marijuana, weed, gas) cost him his job and well his wife, she used that as her opportunity to walk away. Kydee lost everything, his job, his wife, not that he really cared about her for real, and eventually the house. I went to the house before he lost it and visited, even stayed the night a few times. My heart broke for him, but I had his back regardless.

Kydee eventually left the "G" and move to the ATL. We always kept in touch and no matter who either one of us was dealing with, the bond we shared was one that no one could separate. Kydee always seemed to be going through something, always bouncing from female to female as if he was trying to fill a void or something. Through it all he's always said that no one could ever take his love for me away.

After Kydee left and went to the "A" I went back to my ex, Patron, we went through hell back and forth but being the victim of sexual abuse at an early age, it was easier to be with a woman because of my trust issues with men. To be honest, for the life of me I don't know why I give so much of my heart to any man at all when my thought process was tarnished at the precious age of 5.

Anyway, Patron was a stand-up chic, she helped me raise my 2 kids and I never worried about their safety. She loved me, but I think she lowkey felt differently about me because she knew that I was in love with Kydee.

Time would pass by and I wouldn't hear from him for years then he would find a way to get in touch with me usually by his sister Charmaine. You see Charmaine and I lived in the same little small country town and every time I saw her she would tell me, "you know my brother loves you." That ultimately lead to a phone number exchange then our cycle picked up exactly where it left off.

You see when I say my soul was intertwined with this dude to the point where no one could understand our connection, that is an understatement. Thing is, now I wish a million times... no, I don't, I won't say that it was a mistake. I am however hoping that these words will help the next female so that she won't have to deal with the antics of a FCKBoy.

This is one of those moments when Kydee and I haven't heard from each other in a couple of years and he's been dealing with this chic Trina but trust she was far from being the "Baddest Bih."

Anyway, his sister tells me that he's trying to get in touch with me, so once again here we go with the calls and text messages. You see Kydee and I have been cutting (just having sex) all this time but we knew that we had love for each other but it's about to go down because Kydee wants to see if we can make it as a couple and I'm down because all I ever wanted was for us to be together as one.

Although city boy Kydee hates the country he says he loves me enough to come so that we can be together as one, so we move in together. I can't lie our sex game has always been off the Richter scale, me being a pleaser and him enjoying being pleased.

Kydee was a smoker and there were times when we just got high together blunt followed by blunt, but his love for his weeji was more intense for his lust for any woman. That and the fact that he was going back and forth to Atlanta to "handle business" and see his kids, well, that begin to cause problems within our home.

You see Kydee and I had an understanding, I knew that he would be staying with Trina when he went to Atlanta. In fact, she would be the one to send him the money for his ticket to come back and forth. I knew all about Trina because Kydee and I, well, we were friends before anything. I knew all about her, but she didn't know shit about me, she was about to learn today though.

So, as Kydee was packing I told him that there was no trippage (worrying about anything), I knew he was going to fuck while he was there, he's a man and I'm a realist, I just asked that he not put his mouth on her cookie (hot pocket, vagina) and that he wrap it up which I knew was a waste of time, he never use condoms.

You did read earlier in this book that I said that Kydee was given everything within the very depths of my soul, right? I know a lot of you are probably saying damnnnnnnnn she's crazy as hell, truth be told I was in love with the possessor of my soul Kydee. Our connection was like no other, but before anything else I truly believed in our friendship. Sad, sad reality of the situation is now that I look back at everything, our friendship was probably more one-sided.

You see this heart that beats in the center of my chest is somewhat of a curse. My love is truly unconditional, I love to no end and then on top of that I'm a pleaser and I'm loyal, you could never go wrong with me. I've been told that you attract what you put out into the universe, but hell, that can't be true because if that was the situation then I would he happily married. Anyway, enough of that let me tell you how the rest of this plays out.

It's 6:00 a.m. and Kydee was still in Atlanta, I'm in the bed asleep and my cell keeps ringing. I look at the phone it's a 404 number, but I don't know this number. I answer it and there is a female on the other end who I later discover is this chic Trina. Her ass is crying hysterically and I'm thinking damn did something happen to

Kydee. Of course, this is not the situation, she's asking if Kydee is here with me and I instantly begin to laugh at her ass. I ask her how she got my number and she lies and says he gave it to her. My reply was, "and why would he do that?" Then she tells the truth and says that she got it off the little cleaning ticket that was on his clothes. You see Kydee was one of those semi bougie dudes, his clothes had to go into the cleaners unless they were work clothes, yeah that was just him anyway, now that statement was believable.

So, Trina is still on my phone crying and I'm laughing. Is this chic seriously calling my phone? So, I sit up in the middle of my bed and I'm asking her if she knew what time it was, she told me "yes" and asked me again "Is he there with you?" So, then I asked this broad, "Girl are his clothes still there?" she was like "yessssssssssssss", so I was like "then he will be back." As if she thought she was hurting my feelings, she starts telling me that Kydee told her that we were friends and that we were just roommates.

By this time, I'm in my bed rolling around laughing, this chic must be slow. So, I stop laughing long enough to tell her "Yes, we're friends and roommates as well, because we definitely share the same room and bed too."

You see Kydee told me all about this chic and how he met her. She was a friend of his shortie (girlfriend) and how she came over to play cards one night and how they eventually hooked up and started cutting.

Lesson 2

You know he has FCKBoy juice running all through his veins if he's low down enough to creep with his shorty's homie/friend. No matter what the situation is you never, ever, ever shit at the same table you eat from (you never cross that line). Of course, this is only something a FCKBoy would do with no remorse.

Chapter 3

So, Trina is still talking shit, telling me that he's coming home to her and how he wants to be with her and I'm just like ohhhhhhh okay, well Kydee has his own mind so if that's what he wants I can respect that. This chic stop crying in mid sob and says, "WHAT?" I'm like sweetie it's 6:00 o'clock in the morning which means its 5 in Atlanta and you're on my phone calling me, asking me where Kydee is. Come on Ma, he's still in Georgia but he will be at your place soon, then trust me he's coming back to Bama.

You see, we have a connection that surpasses any connection that he has ever made with anyone else. Our souls are intertwined way beyond your comprehension, and her response was "How old are you and you have a fat face?" My response to her was, "old enough and it should be fat I'm pregnant." She started screaming and crying again and I swear I can't stop laughing. That's when I broke it down for her and said, "Look, if you want to keep Kydee you have to do a few things", I don't ask questions I don't want any answers to, I don't go through his phone and I let him be a man.

You see reality is, he's going to fuck no matter what and always know I'm never going anywhere so you will have to accept me because I've been there through the wife and every other female since her. You see, I am the female version of him and he is the male version of me, nothing can ever end this connection not even death."

Hmmmmm yeah, those words were like venom running through her veins and I knew it, so I gave a little bit more just to kill her ego off trying to lowkey come for me. I told her everything about how they met and how she ended screwing her friend's man and that I was nauseated and then I hung up. She kept calling back to back and I kept rejecting her calls and I'm still laughing my ass off because she is so damn stupid, but so was I for accepting this shit because few women would accept these types of shenanigans but ohhh well, I did.

Maybe 10 minutes later passed by and my phone is ringing and Kydee's ringtone is playing, I'm vibing to this song and then I answer. It's that bae Kydee asking me, "Ma you goodie?" I'm like going through the whole little situation giving him all that Georgia Peach tea (gossip, details about a situation) and all he did was apologize and tell me that he would be home soon. We tell each other that we love the other one and he tells me that he will be home soon and then the call ends.

Later that night I met the Greyhound and my King is back in Bama just like I said, so fat-faced and all your girl still makes boss moves. A few weeks later Kydee informs me that he's going to New York with his MA Dukes (mother) so to me it's no big deal, so I help him prepare for his trip.

Kydee leaves for New York and I don't hear from him three weeks straight, but I know that his Uncle Cash is having a big birthday party soon, so I know he will be there. I will see him soon and he's going to feel me when he does.

I order a sexy black and gold dress. You see, Kydee has a thing for cork bottom heels so yeah, I've ordered a gold pair of wedge sandals to match the dress, yeah three weeks huh?

Night of the party I pick up my MA Dukes and then we pick up my Aunt Gee Gee, when my aunt sees me all she says is "Oh wow." Once we get to the party when I say ALL EYES ON ME, especially Kydee, he couldn't stop staring at me, but he kinda kept his distance.

I'm mingling at the party and who do I see? It's his ex-wife Keke. Hmmmmm, so Kydee, is this the reason you're so distant luv?

Lesson 3

There's no excuse to leave home and not keep in touch. If we live under the same roof, you owe me hella respect! I deserve it and I demand it! If he falls off and not touch basis with you when he's out of town, something else is occupying his time. This is definitely the characteristic traits of a FCKBoy.

Chapter 4

Eventually we talk and Kydee tries to explain that he wasn't trying to hurt me. Well luv it sure as hell feels that way, because you definitely didn't respect me. Every time I turned around Kydee's mom was calling him telling him to do this, to do that. I guess she was trying to keep him away from me.

You see, Kydee's mother didn't like me because Kydee and I started messing around at the end of his marriage. To be honest I had only met her once, when he left Trina to move in with me. For the life of me I didn't understand why she was angry with me because it was her son who was a HO! Anyway, all I ever did was love her son and held him down. I mean why is it that people always get mad at the other woman? All we do is go by what the man tells us.

Later that night Kydee and I get away from everyone and I ask him if he's coming over despite everything, I just want a pressure session (sex session) although I'm pissed off and yes this may sound crazy as hell, I'm definitely a sexual being and this is still my man well sort of anyway.

Kydee tells me that he will get someone to drop him off later. We talk for a little while longer and then we go our separate ways back to the party. So many other little petty shit took place that night but I won't waste your time with those details.

Kydee watched me all night long despite the demons that kept riding his back. Truth be told I just wanted to show Kydee everything that he had been missing, even though there wouldn't be a tomorrow for us. Part of me knew that Kydee wouldn't come over that night but everything in me knew that he really wanted to.

I leave the party and go home and yes, I wait on Kydee for a while and then I eventually call him, and he tells me that he still might come over later. If you're wondering if he showed up after all I went through to look absolutely delicious for him, the answer is no.

So, the next morning I go to work and despite how I'm feeling I still wonder what happened. My phone rings and I get excited, it's Kydee wanting to know if I was at home. I was just about to clock out and leave to go home because I thought he was coming to see me. I was still a little fucked off because he didn't show up, but I knew he was about to make it up one way or the other.

He goes on to tell me that he needs to drop some stuff off and pick up a few things, but his words are disregarded, kinda like what he did to my heart. I didn't have time for his ass just like he didn't have time for me the night before. Conversation ends with him telling me that he would be leaving some stuff on my front porch, silence, then nothing. I'm not sure if I hung up or if he did, either way the conversation ended. No closure no answers.

Kydee left all of his belongings at my house and in my heart, I held on to all of them for a long time hoping that eventually he would find his way home. Yeah, I guess at this point you can see that I thoroughly enjoy pain, right? I guess I wasn't aware of the signs that were right there in my face. And even now as I sit here in my bed and I write these words I can't even explain why I kept him in my life all these years.

Kydee's presence in my house always consumed my air and even in his departure with no explanation and now looking at all his shit, baby pictures, birth certificate, social security card, hell my closet is full of his clothes and shoes. Damn, he left all of this? He left me? I literally died on the inside! All the time I'm here dying, guess what his ass is doing? He's living without me.

Reading a post online one day it said, "The Best Way to Get Over One Person Is Under Another One". Hmmmmm, yeah, that's definitely my next move. I wrote this poem and now I need to make a major boss move.

OPERATION MOVE ON

When you left I cried for several days and several nights

Trying to remember the good times, can't forget the fights

All the trips you took outta town every other week

The late-night phone calls, the outta town freaks

You thought I was blind because the sex was fye

Boy kill yaself with that thought let me tell you why...

Every time you left, I knew where you stayed

Every time you went to sleep I knew where you laid

Every time you made a call, I wasn't asleep

Every time you went to da A, yeah, I knew about that freak

Every time you came back, yes, I knew

All the little things your freaky ass would do

Shit you did it to her because you did it with me

Now your ass is gone, finally set me free

Left all your clothes, what you thought you were coming back?

After all you've done, boy you smoking crack?

Now our baby is due the first of the year

Thanks for that blessing.... just cried my last tear.

YEAH, I KNEW

Operation Move on consisted of finding the perfect person to do just that, help me move on. So, I was talking to my homie CJ one day and I asked him about Q. You see Q was a local guy from our lil hometown, on the quiet side but overall a decent person, or so I thought.

CJ went on to tell me that he had hit Q up on social media a few weeks prior to me asking about him. He also told me that Q was doing good for himself, he had a good job and owned his own home, this seems like it's going to be a win-win situation.

So, I find Q on the same social media site and shoot him my number and yes of course he calls. In the process of the calls and texts, Q informs me that he was always attracted to me, but he felt like I was out of his league. I tell him of course he's not and then we decide to go out on a date. Q lives in the "Gump" and I decide to go and visit him for the weekend to take some time and get to know him and that's exactly what I did.

We spent every weekend together and all of this started around October. When Thanksgiving rolled around, Q came and spent Thanksgiving with me at my house. Christmas morning, I've cooked breakfast placed it all on a serving tray and take it to Q who's sitting up in the bed with a big smile on his face. He's nervous for some reason or maybe he's just not use to a woman catering to him.

A few moments later he pulls out a box, hops out of the bed gets down on a bended knee, and he proposes. Two months, yeah, I know, got him! You see, women you walk around every day with two of the most powerful weapons known to man and if you use them right, well sometimes the results can be most beneficial, especially when it's a part of your plan but always remember there are consequences to dishragging anyone, especially if it's for your own personal gain.

After Q and I have breakfast we finish with a lil Pressure Session to celebrate of course. I'm tired but now I have the motivation to go ahead and get rid of Kydee's shit. I go outside and get the big thrash can from out by the road and I start disposing of Kydee's belongings. Some stuff he could never get back or replace but at this point I don't' care, it's over and I'm moving on. Time to start planning this wedding.

Q and I set a date and we decide to get married on my birthday the following year which was September 17th. So, here it is a year later, invitations have been mailed out, dresses and tuxedos ordered, decorations purchased, wedding party selected, my coordinator and venue have both been secured with deposits. I'm really going to do this, I'm going to get married to someone, just not THE ONE, ohhhhhhhh well.

The big day arrives and I'm peeking out into the audience at all of our family and friends who have come to celebrate this union and I look at the alter and I see Q standing there smiling, he's so happy, but reality is my heart isn't really there. Something, no, someone is missing. Of course, I know who it is. Nevermind, I'm getting married today even if it's not him at the altar.

Our wedding and reception was beautiful and now I'm moving to the "Gump" with my new husband. The "Move On Phase" was a complete success. Crazy thing about it though, there was never a Honeymoon Phase. Karma!

A year passes by and I've decided I'm married and I'm going to make the best of my marriage despite everything that was going on behind closed doors. So, Q is working late this particular day and I'm at home alone, so I decided to call Charmaine, Kydee's sister to check on her and the girls Kyriqua and Kyree. We had only been on the phone for about 5 minutes when she started talking about Kydee, of course I tell her that's not why I called but she tells me how hurt he was when he found out I got married, all I'm thinking is, that's what his ass gets.

Then she goes on to tell me that he asked about me when she talked to him earlier. Okay, so here is when the fuckery begins, she tells me to hold for a minute she's getting a beep and then she's like, I will just call you back.

When she did, the first thing she tells me is that her brother wants to talk to me and he told her to give me his number. I'm like nawwww, I'm good but then I decide to tell her to just go ahead and to give him my number. We talk for a little while longer and then we say our goodbyes.

Fifteen minutes later my phone is ringing but this number is not saved in my phone and it's a 678 number, so I automatically know who it is, of course it's Kydee. We talk for a few minutes and now it's at the point where he wants to discuss the fact that I got married. I happily tell him yesssssssssssssss I sure did and then he was like, "Mommie I can't lie, it hurt me when I found out you got married, that was supposed to have been me standing at the alter next to you."

You see all I'm thinking is that he can't be serious, I haven't heard from him in what seems like forever and he's trying to cupcake me, behbi bye!!! The conversation between us does not go well at all and I tell him it doesn't matter anymore, that my husband wants to see him for everything that he put me through, of course, Kydee is not pleased to hear those words so he tells me that my husband definitely doesn't want to see him. Maybe not, but I definitely would like to see them lock up.

Anyway, it would be a few years later after karma has started wreaking havoc in my life that my marriage to Q is at the point of no return. I just want it to be over. All I could say is that Q was a good provider, he took care of the bills, but he was so violent. If I don't get out of this shit this man is going to kill me. Every time we have a disagreement and I try to leave him, he's grabbing his gun and putting it to my head.

You see my well implemented plan is becoming so volatile that its paramount for me to leave his ass as soon as I can. Q served his purpose and now I have to find mine. Over time Kydee and I would find our way back into each other's lives and ultimately end up in this place where I decided to tell you about everything this FCKBoy put me through. Maybe, just maybe this will help you in some type of way.

Just like usual, it starts with the phone calls and the text messages and ultimately the I love yous. This time was different though Kydee is coming harder than he ever has and I'm like, wowwwwwwwwww!

You see, before Kydee made his grand reentrance into my life I was in a good place. I was living the life of celibacy and loving it until I met this absolutely delicious King named Tevin. Tevin broke down barriers in my life that were placed at an early age and although I had love for Kydee the bond that I had with him was somewhat severed because sexually, no one is competing with Tevin. True story, he has my heart, but reality is I know we could never be as one.

Sooooo now I decide to see what Kydee is about all the time thinking, "If you can't be with the one you love, then you should love the one you're with." Kydee and I start talking on the regular and he's saying all of the right words. "Mommie, I can't breathe without you, I'm ready for you to be the end to my story." He's actually discussing marriage on the daily and I'm just like, what the hell? Let's get it!

Lesson 4

If you haven't heard from his ass in a minute and he know that you're in a good place but he's promising all these bullshit ass lies, then please believe me, he's a FCKBoy. He only wants to get you back because he knows that you're a good woman and him, well he's an opportunist. Typical FCKBoy playing FCKBoy games.

Chapter 5

Despite my complete happiness with my situation with Tevin, you do know what happened right? I allowed Kydee to come back and disrupt my entire universe, well to a certain point anyway. Kydee knew all about Tevin because I told him the juicy little details, not to make him jealous, but because reality is, Tevin was the true King in my life and there was no need to deny that.

I knew exactly what Tevin and I shared and it's a situation without a title or any possibility of a future, but that man is just like milk, "he does the body good." Besides it took me a long time for me to trust someone enough to have sex with them and I can honestly say the things that Tevin did to my body filled the void that Kydee and other FCKBoys like him had placed in my life.

Emotionally I got attached to Tevin, I fell in love. Loving Tevin was so simple because he is such an amazing man, a true King with a big heart and of course he's hella sexy. Being with him was probably the only thing in my life that I've done to make me happy. Ummmmmm, ummmmm the thoughts of the last time I had a pressure session with Tevin is making my body ache for his presence right now.

No matter how the connection is with Tevin, Kydee and I have history and I felt like he owed me his whole life, especially after he had consumed and digested the contents of mine. Kydee and I make plans for him to come for a visit, just so we can see if we can make this lifetime thing a reality. It took a minute to work out the details because I swear Kydee was always having financial problems. I never understood what the problem was for real, if it was his drug habit of the fact that he was paying child support for 5 kids. I'm not sure but I swear it had me a little pressed. Every time I turned around Kydee was always calling to borrow money until his payday, yeah, so you think I'm stupid at this point correct?

Well I am a true Queen and a Queen holds her King down despite his downfalls or if he's fallen on bad times and he's down on his dick, it's always her responsibility to uplift him. It's kind of crazy if you think about it, but just in case you missed it earlier I'll tell you again, I'm a pleaser inside the bed and out. I swear I hate this heart that beats in the lower left side of my chest sometimes it seems more like a curse than the center of my being.

Lesson 5

If he comfortably asks you for money on the regular, then trust me, he's definitely a FCKBoy! Trust me, a real man would rather go without than to ask a woman for money, it bruises his ego to have to depend on a woman or ask a woman for anything and furthermore if he can't stand on his own two feet, ten toes down without begging for money from the chic he calls "Mommie, Ma or Queen", trust me, this boy has FCK in front of his title.

Chapter 6

Now Kydee is making plans to come for a weekend but he must make plans around his current living situation. You see this is where the truth finally comes out. Kydee really lives in Atlanta with Trina, oh shit now everything makes sense. All the late-night texting and the walks to the store to get coffee, these were the windows of opportunity to call me, hmmmmm.

Kydee explains that it's over and that he has already told Trina, but he stays there because he doesn't really have anywhere else to stay and besides that they worked at the same distribution center together. Now that I think back, it seems like a bunch of bullshit, but even the biggest liar tells the truth sometimes and he definitely had his game face on.

Kydee kept insisting that Trina was outdated, one that should have never happened from the beginning. So, I decided to give him just one more chance despite the fact that my woman's intuition was telling me to fall back, all the way back. My connection with him made me want him, besides he was talking about marriage every single day, maybe just maybe he was ready.

Kydee would often tell me that this would be our first marriage because he should have never married Keke, especially after catching her in the bed with another man the day before the wedding. My marriages either because he knew I didn't marry Geno or Q because I really loved them.

You see Kydee and I, we were the best of friends, we discussed any and everything. He knew all of my secrets and I was given the key to his soul a long time ago and all of these things were written in stone from the very beginning.

So, I decide to embrace this thing that I think is love.

Anyway, the weekend is finally here and Kydee is on his way. I'm looking in the mirror and I barely recognize myself, your girl is extra saucy, and my nerves are in a complete wreck. You see it's been 5 years since I've seen Kydee in the flesh and of course we have some making up to do.

Kydee is coming into Montgomery so I put my bags in the car and leave home beating the interstate and one my favorite artist DJ Luke Nasty comes on and I'm vibing, "Doing 80 in a 60 fuck a ticket, cause I ain't had that pussy in a minute, ayeeeeeee, I'm on the way." Needless to say, when Kydee saw me all he could do is lick his lips, stare, and of course he couldn't keep his hands off me.

We get to the hotel and we check in and head to the elevator. We kissing, licking, rubbing, touching, he's hard and I'm dripping from anticipation. As soon as we enter the room we dropping bags, clothes hitting the floor and the session begins. After we're finished we both take a shower and prepare for our date. Kydee rolls a blunt while I get dressed and we talk about the situation with Trina. Kydee explains that we have to plan his escape plane out perfectly because Trina is all about drama and he wants to get away from her as soon as possible and make me his wife. Me, I'm just ready to get this behbi to the house, or so I thought.

Kydee kept his phone powered off because Trina was the clingy type of chic. Personally, I never worried about another female especially when it came to Kydee because I was there through the wifey, the girlfriends, and the slide-by-nights. No one could ever take my place. Now that I look back at the situation that shit wasn't a privilege it was more like a pitiful ass situation which leads me to the next lesson.

<u>*Lesson 6*</u>

If he is in a situation that he constantly complains about and he's always telling you that he's not happy and that that he wants to build a future with you, but he wants you to just be patient for a minute while he comes up with an "escape plan", trust me he's a FCKBoy!

Reality of the situation is, no <u>REAL</u> man starts another situation without first ending the one he's in. He's not trying to build with you at all, he's being selfish, he knows he has something real he just knows nothing about being real himself.

Chapter 7

Later that night after several more pressure sessions, Kydee is laying there asleep and I'm up texting Tevin. Yes, I'm in love with Tevin but with us, what's understood will never have to be explained. I tell him that I love him, but I've decided to see if I can build a future with Kydee. Ladies never let good sex interfere with your common sense, epic failure.

Tevin tells me that he understands, and we exchange a few other comments and I end our conversation letting him know that I will always love him, and he tells me that he will always be there for me. Now the journey begins, true story it ends just as fast as it begins. A couple of months pass by and Kydee arrives but when he shows up he doesn't even have a bag, I'm like wtf! It's coolish though, I'm a Queen by all rights and I got him. So, the next day we go shopping, I grabbed him some clothes and personal items, I had to make sure he had what he needed. I should have seen that fuckery when it was playing out, he wasn't even remotely ready to be a King even though I treated him like one.

Kydee only wanted to do the same thing every day, smoke his weeji, get the munchies, eat, and of course sex. He said he was looking for a job, but he only searched at the temporary agencies which brought up a big red flag for me. There were hundreds of positions in the vicinity of our townhouse, but he kept looking for temporary positions. Hmmmmm, I did tell you about a woman's intuition, right? Temporary job=Temporary situation. This could be a lesson but just pay attention to the situation at hand. If he's planning to build a future with you then why the hell is he seeking part-time work?

He finally got a job and every single day he came home to a hot meal, a clean house, and a good woman. A true King would have appreciated this, but not Kydee, he was selfish and no matter what I did it just wasn't enough for him. Every day with him was miserable. Things were not the same between us and I was in love with another man and it was my thoughts of Tevin that got me through the little pressure sessions I was having with Kydee and the first time I called Tevin's name while we were having sex, there was no coming back from that.

I started sleeping in my daughter's room or on the couch. At this point I just want him gone and I keep telling him to leave and he kept telling me that he didn't have anywhere else to go and he promises that he's going to do better. I listen but truth is I'm over it and him too.

Lesson 7

If he lacks the ability to be the King of his castle and he's always looking for a temporary solution to his situation, trust me he's also looking for a way out and you're nothing more than a pitstop. See it for what it is and not for what he looks into your eyes and tells you it is, he's lying trust me. Nothing more than the tactics of a FCKBoy.

Chapter 8

The way that Kydee is set up all the signs were there from the beginning. Silly me, I was too blind to see him for who he really was until he started dealing with Kresha. This man went from taking a bath 3 times a day, lotioning down from head to toe with Palmer's Coconut lotion, making sure the house stayed clean, washing clothes every other day, to living in an apartment with Kresha. She was a dirty foot bottom dweller who lives in a damn near condemned apartment complex that is beyond filthy and it has no glass in the windows in the bedrooms just cardboard.

You see Kydee doesn't work, he actually just gave her his info so that she could put him on her food stamps and Kresha, she's just happy to say he lives there with her. Now please don't get it twisted I'm not salty, I'm going to make a valid point in a few seconds, trust me my life has definitely improved since Kydee left to be honest, I've never been more complete.

In the beginning I blamed myself for the demise of our relationship, damn near felt like I wasn't good enough for him, but the reality of the situation is that he was never worthy of me, so...

Lesson 8

It's simple but I really need you to understand this. Ladies always know your worth, never let your crown tilt for anyone. If he makes a drastic change in his life and he go from your Suga to her Shit, trust me he was nothing more than a facade, he was a FCKBoy in grown man's clothing that you probably purchased.

His attempt to dishrag you reflect his inner incompetence and he probably has "mommy issues" and lacks the ability to be a real man. Don't ever blame yourself for not seeing what it was the entire time. It was never your fault, he *was destined to be a FCKBoy before he came out of his mother's womb and he will forever be Kydee the FCKBoy.*

Kydee's
Karma

Kydee is a nonfictional person with fictitious characteristic traits who creeped into my thought process like a thief in the night and stole my heart and left an agonizing void that now has been filled with peace.

True story, Kydee's entire existence is one of complete fuckery. Ladies never should you dumb down to please another person. In life we all encounter some type of predator telling us that they love and adore us. Reality is they prey on you because they know of your undying loyalty, that your heart is genuine, and they know that they can manipulate your emotions and completely dominate your existence, and these are the things to be aware of and are the signs of an FCKBoy.

Now as far as why I chose 8 lessons, it's simple. The number for infinity is 8 and the meaning for infinity can be "endlessness or limitlessness" and the number 8 also relates to the concept of Karma, which means a FCKBoy should face infinite Karma for this lifetime and the next 8 lifetimes and I will always and forever be

~Kydee's Karma~

www.ingramcontent.com/pod-product-compliance
Lightning Source LLC
Chambersburg PA
CBHW030529260626
47157CB00005B/1948